DANGEROUS CATS™

TIGERS
World's Largest Cats

Amelie von Zumbusch

PowerKiDS press

New York

For Julianna Maria Sophia

Published in 2007 by The Rosen Publishing Group, Inc.
29 East 21st Street, New York, NY 10010

First Edition

Book Design: Erica Clendening
Layout Design: Julio Gil
Photo Researcher: Sam Cha

Photo Credits: Cover, pp. 1, 14, 16, 20 © www.shutterstock.com; pp. 4, 8 © www.istockphoto.com/eROMAZe; p. 6 © www.istockphoto.com/Paul Wolf; p. 10 © www.istockphoto.com/Stephanie Kuwasaki; p. 12 © Digital Stock; p. 18 © Digital Vision

Library of Congress Cataloging-in-Publication Data

Zumbusch, Amelie von.
  Tigers : world's largest cats / Amelie von Zumbusch. — 1st ed.
      p. cm. — (Dangerous cats)
  Includes index.
  ISBN-13: 978-1-4042-3632-5 (library binding)
  ISBN-10: 1-4042-3632-5 (library binding)
  1. Tigers—Juvenile literature. I. Title.
  QL737.C23Z799 2007
  599.756—dc22
                                    2006019556

Manufactured in the United States of America

Contents

The Tiger

Tigers are one of the four kinds of great cats. Lions, leopards, and jaguars are the other great cats. Only great cats, such as the tiger, can roar. Great cats are bigger than other cats are. The tiger is the largest cat in the world.

The tiger is one of the few cats that like to swim. Tigers that live in hot places swim often. Swimming helps these tigers stay cool.

Tigers are very good swimmers. They can swim for over 15 miles (24 km).

A Striped Cat

Tigers are powerful animals. They most often weigh between 150 and 650 pounds (68–295 kg).

Most tigers have orange coats with dark stripes. However, tigers can also have white coats with dark stripes. Each tiger has a different **pattern** of stripes. **Scientists** can tell one tiger from another by looking at their stripes.

White tigers have blue eyes. Orange tigers have yellow eyes. All tigers have good eyesight. Tigers can also see very well at night.

The tiger is the only great cat that has stripes.

Where Tigers Live

Tigers live in Asia. They can be found in India, China, Indonesia, Southeast Asia, and eastern Russia.

Nearly all tigers live in forests. However, tigers can live in many different kinds of forests. Some tigers live in **rain forests**. Other tigers live in drier forests. Some tigers live in snowy, **coniferous forests**.

Tigers always live near water. They need lots of water to drink. Tigers also swim in water to cool off.

This tiger lives in the Ranthambore National Park in Rajasthan, India.

Kinds of Tigers

Scientists often list tigers in different **subspecies**. The subspecies of tigers living today include Sumatran tigers, South China tigers, Amur tigers, Bengal tigers, and Indo-Chinese tigers.

Sumatran tigers live on the Indonesian island of Sumatra. They are the smallest tigers. Sumatran tigers have dark orange coats and many black stripes.

Amur tigers live in eastern Russia, China, and North Korea. The winters are very cold there. Amur tigers have thick coats to keep them warm.

Most Bengal tigers live in India. Bengal tigers are the most common subspecies of tiger.

Tigers are **predators**. They most often eat large, four-legged animals. Their favorite **prey** is wild pigs, wild cows, and deer. However, they will also eat fish, birds, and other small animals.

A tiger hides behind bushes, trees, or tall grasses and creeps up on its prey. When the tiger is close, it jumps on the prey and kills it. The tiger eats its fill of meat. The tiger hides any leftover meat to eat later.

Tigers most often hunt between sunset and sunrise.

Tiger Cubs

Baby tigers are called cubs. A mother tiger most often has two or three cubs at a time. When tiger cubs are born, they weigh about 2.2 pounds (1 kg). Cubs are born with their eyes closed. After a week or two, the cubs' eyes open and they can see.

Tiger cubs drink their mother's milk until they are about six months old. At six to eight weeks old, they start to eat meat.

Tiger cubs get their first set of teeth when they are about five weeks old. As they grow older, the cubs lose their baby teeth and get adult teeth, just as people do.

Growing Up

Tiger cubs spend much of their time playing and **wrestling** with each other. The cubs gain important skills by playing. They also learn a lot by watching their mother.

Tiger cubs most often stay with their mother until they are between 18 and 30 months old. They then go off to find **territories** of their own. The daughters often find territories near their mother's territory. The sons find territories farther away.

Tiger cubs like to wrestle, chase each other, and climb trees. These tiger cubs are climbing a tree at a zoo in Bhopal, India.

Tiger Territories

Except for mother tigers that are caring for their cubs, adult tigers spend almost all their time alone. Each adult tiger has its own territory, where it lives and hunts.

Tigers have several ways of marking their territory. They roar to let other tigers know where they are. They use their strong claws to make **scratches** on trees. Tigers even rub their **scent glands** on trees to let other tigers know that they were there.

A tiger's territory is generally between 8 and 200 square miles (21–518 sq km). Tigers that live in places with less prey have larger territories.

Tiger Attacks

Tigers generally stay away from people. However, a tiger will **attack** a person if it is afraid that person will hurt its cubs. Some tigers even hunt people for food. These tigers are called man-eaters. Tigers often become man-eaters because they are too old or sick to catch other prey.

Some people who live near man-eating tigers wear masks on the backs of their heads. This fools the tigers, who attack their prey from behind.

Tigers have sharp, strong teeth. Their big teeth are generally 2.5 to 3 inches (6.4–7.6 cm) long.

An Endangered Cat

Tigers are **endangered**. Scientists who study tigers believe that there are only between 5,000 and 7,500 tigers living in the wild today.

One reason tigers are endangered is because people hunt them. People sell the tigers' fur, teeth, and other body parts. Another problem tigers face is that they have lost much of their land to people. People who need a place to live and farm often take over land where tigers live.

Glossary

attack (uh-TAK) To start a fight with.

coniferous forests (kah-NIH-fur-us FOR-ests) Forests with trees that have cones and needlelike leaves.

endangered (in-DAYN-jerd) Describing a kind of animal that has almost died out.

pattern (PA-turn) The way colors and shapes appear over and over again on something.

predators (PREH-duh-terz) Animals that kill other animals for food.

prey (PRAY) Animals that are hunted by other animals for food.

rain forests (RAYN FOR-ests) Thick forests that receive a large amount of rain during the year.

scent glands (SENT GLANDZ) Body parts that make a smell that animals use to mark their land.

scientists (SY-un-tists) People who study the world.

scratches (SKRACH-ez) Rubs or tears.

subspecies (SUB-spee-sheez) Different kinds of the same animal.

territories (TER-uh-tor-eez) Lands or spaces that animals guard for their use.

wrestling (REH-sul-ing) Struggling or fighting with.

Index

Web Sites

Due to the changing nature of Internet links, PowerKids Press has developed an online list of Web sites related to this book. This site is updated regularly. Please use this link to access the list:
www.powerkidslinks.com/dcats/tigers/